Please return or renew this item before the latest date shown below

SM

10/22

St Monans

Renewals can be made
by internet   www.onfife.com/fife-libraries
in person   at any library in Fife
by phone   03451 55 00 66

ON
AT FIFE
LIBRARIES

Thank you for using your library

In memory of our first editor, Elke Lacey,
and for her son, Fred.

First published 1993 by Methuen Children's Books
This edition published 2016 by Macmillan Children's Books
an imprint of Pan Macmillan
The Smithson, 6 Briset Street, London EC1M 5NR
EU representative: Macmillan Publishers Ireland Limited,
1st Floor, The Liffey Trust Centre,
117-126 Sheriff Street Upper, Dublin 1, D01 YC43

Associated companies throughout the world
www.panmacmillan.com

ISBN 978-1-5098-0478-8

Text copyright © Julia Donaldson 1993
Illustrations copyright © Axel Scheffler 1993, 2003

The right of Julia Donaldson and Axel Scheffler to be identified
as the author and illustrator of this work has been asserted by them
in accordance with the Copyright, Designs and Patents Act 1988.

13 15 14 12

A CIP catalogue record for this book is available
from the British Library.

Printed in China

WRITTEN BY
JULIA DONALDSON

ILLUSTRATED BY
AXEL SCHEFFLER

A Squash and a Squeeze

MACMILLAN CHILDREN'S BOOKS

A little old lady lived all by herself
With a table and chairs and a jug on the shelf.

A wise old man heard her grumble and grouse,
"There's not enough room in my house.
Wise old man, won't you help me, please?
My house is a squash and a squeeze."

"Take in your hen," said the wise old man.

"Take in my hen? What a curious plan."

Well, the hen laid an egg on the fireside rug,

And flapped round the room knocking over the jug.

The little old lady cried, "What shall I do?
It was poky for one and it's tiny for two.
My nose has a tickle and there's no room to sneeze.
My house is a squash and a squeeze."

And she said, "Wise old man,
       won't you help me, please?
My house is a squash and a squeeze."

"Take in your goat," said the wise old man.

"Take in my goat? What a curious plan."

Well, the goat chewed the curtains and trod on the egg,

then sat down to nibble the table leg.

The little old lady cried, "Glory be!
It was tiny for two and it's titchy for three.
The hen pecks the goat and the goat's got fleas.
My house is a squash and a squeeze."

And she said, "Wise old man,
      won't you help me, please?
My house is a squash and a squeeze."

"Take in your pig," said the wise old man.

"Take in my pig? What a curious plan."

So she took in her pig who kept chasing the hen,

And raiding the larder again and again.

The little old lady cried, "Stop, I implore!
It was titchy for three and it's teeny for four.
Even the pig in the larder agrees,
My house is a squash and a squeeze."

And she said, "Wise old man,
        won't you help me, please?
My house is a squash and a squeeze."

"Take in your cow," said the wise old man.

"Take in my cow? What a curious plan."

Well, the cow took one look and charged straight at the pig,
Then jumped on the table and tapped out a jig.

The little old lady cried, "Heavens alive!
It was teeny for four and it's weeny for five.
I'm tearing my hair out, I'm down on my knees.
My house is a squash and a squeeze."

And she said, "Wise old man,
        won't you help me, please?
My house is a squash and a squeeze."

"Take them all out," said the wise old man.
"But then I'll be back where I first began."

So she opened the window and out flew the hen.
"That's better – at last I can sneeze again."

She shooed out the goat and she shoved out the pig.
"My house is beginning to feel pretty big."

She huffed and she puffed and she pushed out the cow.
"Just look at my house, it's enormous now.

"Thank you, old man, for the work you have done.
It was weeny for five, it's gigantic for one.
There's no need to grumble and there's no need to grouse.
There's plenty of room in my house."

And now she's full of frolics and fiddle-de-dees.
It isn't a squash and it isn't a squeeze.

Yes, she's full of frolics and fiddle-de-dees.
It isn't a squash or a squeeze.